Frog's Breathtaking Speech

By the same author

Sitting on a Chicken
The Best (Ever) 52 Yoga Games to Teach in Schools
Michael Chissick
Illustrated by Sarah Peacock
ISBN 978 1 84819 325 3
eISBN 978 0 85701 280 7

Seahorse's Magical Sun Sequences
How all children (and sea creatures) can use yoga to
feel positive, confident and completely included
Michael Chissick
Illustrated by Sarah Peacock
ISBN 978 1 84819 283 6
eISBN 978 0 85701 230 2

Ladybird's Remarkable Relaxation
How children (and frogs, dogs, flamingos and dragons) can use yoga
relaxation to help deal with stress, grief, bullying and lack of confidence
Michael Chissick
Illustrated by Sarah Peacock
ISBN 978 1 84819 146 4
eISBN 978 0 85701 112 1

Frog's Breathtaking Speech

How Children (and Frogs) Can Use Yoga Breathing to Deal with Anxiety, Anger and Tension

Written by Michael Chissick

Illustrated by Sarah Peacock

SINGING
DRAGON
LONDON AND PHILADELPHIA

First published in 2012
by Singing Dragon
an imprint of Jessica Kingsley Publishers
73 Collier Street
London N1 9BE, UK
and
400 Market Street, Suite 400
Philadelphia, PA 19106, USA

www.singingdragon.com

Library of Congress Cataloging in Publication Data
A CIP catalog record for this book is available from the Library of Congress

British Library Cataloguing in Publication Data
A CIP catalogue record for this book is available from the British Library

ISBN 978 1 84819 091 7
eISBN 978 0 85701 074 2

Printed and bound in China

This book is dedicated to:

Nobuyo, Claire and Andrew – breathtaking people in my life

MC

Rob – my wonderful husband

SP

Acknowledgements

I would like to thank the head teachers who had the courage and belief to allow yoga in their schools as part of the integrated school day. Thanks to them, *Frog's Breathtaking Speech* has grown and developed into an activity that has helped, and will continue to help, hundreds of children deal with stressful aspects of their lives.

In particular I would like to express my immense gratitude to:

Karen Scudamore, Head of Holdbrook Primary School, Waltham Cross, Hertfordshire.

Sarah Goldsmith, Head of Downfield Primary School, Cheshunt, Hertfordshire.

Lynda Pritchard, Head of Warren Primary School, Thurrock, Essex.

A big thank you to Veronica Armson deputy head teacher of Phoenix School who made all this possible.

I would also like to say an enormous thank you to all the class teachers, teaching assistants and learning support assistants who I work with week in and week out. Without whom none of this is possible.

Finally, thank you to all the children who roared, hummed, HAAAAAA'd and continue to breathe through their noses to stay calm.

Guidance for Teachers

Introduction

Frog's Breathtaking Speech is aimed at primary and elementary school teachers, head teachers, teaching assistants and people in the field of special needs who may have little or no knowledge of yoga, as well as children's yoga teachers, and is suitable for children of all ages.

School teachers will find the postures and breathing techniques simple to teach and will enjoy their introduction to the fascinating subject of breathing. Children's yoga teachers will broaden and enrich their teaching and will save hours of planning.

I have been using *Frog's Breathtaking Speech* in children's yoga lessons for many years. The story grew out of the need to increase children's awareness of their breath and, more importantly, how to apply it in stressful situations. Situations such as dealing with exams, spelling and table tests, being bullied, tension, headaches and anger, and of course performing or presenting to their peers and parents in assembly.

How to use this book

The story can easily be integrated into your provision for self-esteem enhancement, for example, SEAL, PSHE or Circle Time in the UK.

The story highlights four breathing strategies for dealing with:

- anxiety
- tension and voice development
- tension and headaches
- anger.

Read the story to your class and invite them to talk about situations when they have experienced anger, anxiety or tension. Of course actions speak louder than words so as quickly as you can, please, start the calming crocodile breath, roar the school down with the lion, enjoy the gentle vibration of the humming bee, and, finally, blast out your breath in the woodchopper. You will discover immediately that the children love the activities and the postures because they are fun, achievable and meaningful.

The best strategy is to use the story in a yoga/drama lesson. I usually set out the yoga mats in a circle in the hall. I am sure you will improvise if you do not have mats. You do not have to stick rigidly to the story; feel free to adapt, change and improve. In fact, I would encourage you to go into the drama knowing the story inside out and with a few notes of the story line to hand as a guide. That way you can keep an eye on the action and the behaviour.

Try to give as many children as possible the opportunity to be Frog. Ask for sad faces and then ask for less sad faces as the story unfolds. The other characters, Crocodile, Lion, Humming Bee and Mr Gumble the Woodchopper, are normally the whole class. To keep the "chorus" in unison I hold up placards in pantomime style saying, "Why so sad Frog?" and "I know an interesting way to breathe."

Another approach that has proved very successful is to perform the piece on the school stage. You can select children to play the main characters while the rest of the class are positioned on the floor around the stage. They can reinforce the breathing activities and postures by performing them at the appropriate time. Choose a suitable child to be the narrator, make sure actors know their lines and that the performance takes on great pace and therefore more audience interest. On some occasions I have seen amazing audience participation. Great fun, but be prepared for lots of noise. Several of my classes have given terrific performances to peers and parents. Keep costumes and props simple. I have found that masks work well.

Do enjoy the characters. The Lion is an obvious favourite; children simply love being given permission to make loads of noise.

You might want to try roaring very softly and then very loudly and then somewhere in the middle. The same will apply to the Humming Bee.

What comes first?

I am often asked whether it is best to teach the postures and techniques first and then get stuck into the story. Well, I have tried several different approaches and have found for me and the children that I teach that behaviour and concentration is better when you teach the postures and techniques as the story unfolds. Be prepared to be flexible and do experiment to discover what works best in each situation.

Whatever your approach have fun and please keep reminding the children how these skills and breathing techniques can help them through all kinds of challenges.

Learning objectives

By the end of three or four sessions most of the children will be able to say:

- I know how to calm myself using the Crocodile Breath.

- I know that I can use the Humming Bee Breath when I have a tense headache.

- I know how to use the Woodchopper Breath to get rid of anger.

- I know how to practise the Lion Breath to make my voice stronger.

One warm, sunny afternoon the Frog sat by the river's edge

looking very,
very,
very,
very sad.

Along came his friend Crocodile.

When Crocodile looked
at Frog's face, he asked:

"Why so sad, Frog?"

Frog replied:

"I'll tell you why
I'm so sad.

Tomorrow morning, at Frog School, I have to make a speech about breathing. I don't know much about breathing and I am very,

very,

very,

very scared."

Crocodile listened carefully, smiled, and said:
"I know an interesting way to breathe.
This is what I do.

I breathe IN through my nose.

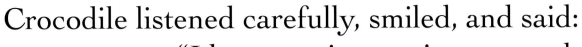

Then I breathe OUT through my nose."

"Frog, I would say that this is a *very* interesting way to breathe, because when you breathe slowly and carefully in and out of your nose it calms you down.

Which means if you are worried, anxious or even frightened about something, this way of breathing will help you deal with it better.

I am very proud of this way of breathing. I call it the Crocodile Breath."

"I see," said Frog, "that is an interesting way to breathe.
I think I will make a note about it in my note pad."

"Thank you, Crocodile," said Frog.

"You are welcome," replied Crocodile and he slid down the river.

Frog finished his notes and continued to sit by the river's edge, looking sad, although not quite as sad as he had been.

Along came his friend Lion.

When Lion looked at
Frog's face, he asked:

"Why so sad, Frog?"

Frog replied: "I'll tell you why I'm so sad. Tomorrow morning, at Frog School, I have to make a speech about breathing. I don't know much about breathing and I am very,

very,

very scared."

Lion listened carefully, smiled, and said:

"I know an interesting way to breathe.
This is what I do. I breathe IN through my nose.
Then I roar OUT through my mouth, like this."

And with that he stretched apart each of his claws,
raised his eyebrows, opened his jaw as wide as he could,
stuck out his long pink tongue as far as it would go

and let out the most
enormous roar you
have ever heard.

"Frog, I would say that this is a *very* interesting way to breathe, because when you roar your breath out like that it helps to loosen your jaw, especially if your jaw has been feeling tense or tight.

Also, if you practice this breath your voice will become stronger and louder. This is good news because it means that teachers will stop saying *"Speak up – I can't hear you."*

I am very proud of this way of breathing. I call it the Lion Breath."

"I see," said Frog, "that is an interesting way to breathe. I will make a note about it in my note pad.

Thank you, Lion."

"You are welcome," replied the Lion and he slinked off into the meadow.

Frog finished his notes and continued to sit by the river's edge, looking sad, although not quite as sad as before.

Along came his friend Humming Bee.

When Humming Bee looked
at Frog's face, he asked:

"Why so sad, Frog?"

Frog replied: "I'll tell you why I'm so sad.

Tomorrow morning, at Frog School, I have to make a speech about breathing. I don't know much about breathing and I am very,

very scared."

Humming Bee listened carefully, smiled, and said:

"I know an interesting way to breathe. This is what I do. I breathe IN through my nose. Then I hum the breath OUT through my mouth. Like this."

And with that he expanded his chest like a balloon as he breathed in through his nose. Effortlessly he began to hum as he breathed out through his mouth.

Hmmmmmmmmmmmmmmmmm

"If I run out of breath I just start again." With that he expanded his chest again and as he breathed out he hummed even louder *and longer* than before.

"Frog, I would say that this is a *very* interesting way to breathe," hummed the Humming Bee, "because when you hum it helps headaches go away.

If you don't have a headache humming is a fun thing to do.

I am very proud of this way of breathing. I call it the Humming Bee Breath."

"I see," said Frog, "that is an interesting way to breathe. I will make a note about it in my note pad.

Thank you, Humming Bee."

"You are welcome," replied the Humming Bee
and he buzzed off to the poppy field.

Frog finished his notes and continued to sit by the river's
edge, looking sad, although a lot less sad than before.

Along came his friend Mr Gumble the Woodchopper.

When Mr Gumble
looked at Frog's
face, he asked:

"Why so sad, Frog?"

Frog replied: "I'll tell you why I'm so sad.

Tomorrow morning, at
Frog School, I have to make
a speech about breathing.

I don't know
much about
breathing and
I am very scared."

Mr Gumble listened carefully, smiled, and said:
"I know an interesting way to breathe. This is what
I do. I stand straight with my feet apart. Then I raise
my axe over my head keeping my arms straight.

As I raise my axe over my head I take a deep breath IN through
my nose. Then, as I bring my axe down towards the space
between my feet, I cry OUT *'Haaaaaa'* as fiercely as I can."

And with that he raised his axe over his head, breathing in through his nose.

Then he brought his axe down towards the space between his feet, crying out *"Haaaaaa"* with all his might.

"Frog, I would say that this is a *very* interesting way to breathe," said Mr Gumble, "especially when you are angry.

This is because when you use the *Haaaaaa* breath any anger that is trapped inside of you is allowed to escape. When your anger has escaped you feel calm and happy again.

I am very proud of this way of breathing. I call it the Woodchopper Breath."

"I see," said Frog, "that is an interesting way to breathe. I will make a note about it in my note pad. Thank you, Mr Gumble."

"You are welcome," replied Mr Gumble and he trudged off to the forest.

Frog gathered his notes and hopped home as
fast as his green legs could carry him.

He went straight to his room, sat at his desk and, using
the notes, carefully wrote the speech. It was a challenge
for him, but soon he had completed the work.

Next morning he woke up, dressed quickly in his best
Frogs School uniform and hopped off to school.

As he stood by the door that led into
the hall, he peered through the glass.

There in the hall, waiting to hear his speech,
were three hundred frog school children.

Frog felt more
than nervous.

He felt more
than anxious.

He felt more
than worried.

He was soooooooooo
oooooooooooooooo
ooooooooo scared.

His hands were
clammy and he
could feel butterflies
in his tummy.

"Oh dear," he
wondered, "will I
be able to talk?"

"What shall I do
to calm myself?"
he asked himself.

Shall I do the
Lion Breath?

Or shall I do the
Humming Bee Breath?

Maybe the
Woodchopper Breath?

Perhaps the
Crocodile Breath?

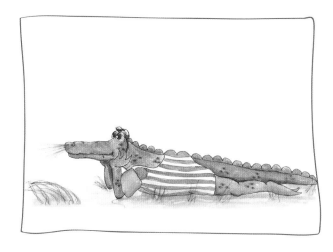

Frog made his decision: "I'll choose the Crocodile Breath," he thought, "that's the one to settle me."

He stood outside the hall, slowly and carefully breathing in and out of his nose for a full five minutes.

When at last he felt calm enough, he strode into the hall confidently. The place fell silent as the three hundred frog children stared at him, waiting.

Frog cleared his throat
and began his speech.

At that moment
all anxiety seemed
to disappear.

He felt brave enough to
look at his audience and
only needed to glance at
his notes once or twice.

"Gosh," he thought to
himself, more than a little
surprised, "they look as if
they are enjoying this!"

As indeed they were.

The hall was stunningly silent.

No one moved.

No one hopped.

No one spoke.

No one fidgeted.

You could hear a pin drop, except of course for the sound of Frog's voice.

"…and that is why I think breathing *is* an interesting subject. Thank you for listening," Frog said, finishing his speech.

Suddenly an explosion of clapping filled the hall.

As the clapping gradually faded the Head Frog
Teacher hopped to the front of the hall and spoke:

"Frog you have made a wonderful speech today. We could hear
every word, it was enjoyable and interesting and you told us
amazing things about breathing that will help us have better lives.
It is an honour to present you with this certificate."

Frog looked proudly at the golden certificate
in his webbed hands. It read:
Frog's Breathtaking Speech.

He thought for a moment how he had changed his sadness to
happiness. He felt strong inside knowing that if problems came
his way, he could at least solve some of them by using his breath.

Helpful Guidance on the Postures and Breathing Techniques

Crocodile Posture to accompany Crocodile Breath

(Known in yoga circles as *Makarasana*.)

- Lie flat on your tummy.
- Elbows as close together as possible.
- Hands supporting chin.
- Gentle curve in your back.

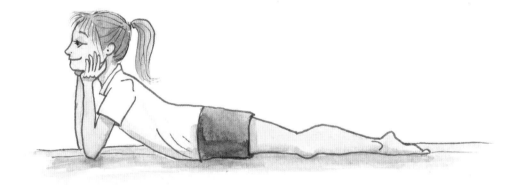

Secret ingredient: Add a big crocodile *calm* smile.

Frog Posture

(Known in yoga circles as a Kneeling Squat.)

- Squat with your knees apart.
- Position your arms between your knees hands flat on the floor if possible.

Secret ingredient: Start with a miserable face and finish with a smile.

Lion Breath

(Known in yoga circles as a *Simhasana*.)

- Find yourself in a kneeling position.

- Breathe in through your nose; breathe out roaring through your mouth.

- Have your fingers stretched apart, eyebrows stretching upwards, mouth as wide as can be, and tongue stretching out and downwards as far as it will go.

Secret ingredient: Roar loudly, then softly, then somewhere in the middle.

Humming Bee Breath

(Known in yoga circles as *Bhramani Pranayama*.)

- Stand with your feet apart or sit crossed legged or kneeling.

- Breathe in through your nose and hum as you breathe out through your mouth.

Secret ingredient: Try it with eyes closed and ears covered. See who can breathe out for longest. Try humming loudly, then very softly, then somewhere in the middle.

Woodchopper Breath

(Known in yoga circles as *Kashtha Takshanasana*, this is adapted for children.)

- Stand with your feet apart.

- Breathe in through your nose, pretending to bring an axe up and over your head.

- On the out breath pretend to bring the axe down towards the ground, allowing yourself a mighty HAAAAAAAAAA breath.

Secret ingredient: Try loudly, then softly and then somewhere in the middle.

Michael Chissick has been teaching yoga to children in primary mainstream and special needs schools as part of the integrated school day since 1999. He is a leading specialist in teaching yoga to children with autistic spectrum disorders (ASD). Michael continues to train and mentor students who want to teach yoga to children, and is well known as 'The Teachers' Teacher'. Michael is acknowledged by the yoga community and the education sector as a genuine leader in this field.

Michael is happy to give advice and guidance about teaching and training to anyone involved in teaching yoga to children. Contact info@yogaatschool.org.uk or visit the website www.yogaatschool.org.uk.

Sarah Peacock's delightful characterisation of Frog and his friends are typical examples of her unique talent. Her illustrations are detailed, fun, story enhancing and reflect the moods of each character. Following a first class degree in Theatre Design, Sarah then completed her teacher training in 2004. Her passion for art and illustration are in abundant evidence around the Hertfordshire primary school where she teaches; enhancing not only the school environment, but also providing inspiration to the children.

You can contact Sarah at sarahpeacock30@yahoo.co.uk.